SUPER SWITCH

Adapted by Heather Alexander

Based on the series created by Todd J. Greenwald

Part One is based on the episode, "Disenchanted Evening," Written by Jack Sanderson

Part Two is based on the episode, "Report Card," Written by Gigi McCreery & Perry Rein & Peter Murrieta

DISNEY PRESS

New York

PART ONE

Chapter One

Alex Russo slowly pulled a brush through her long, wavy brown hair. She gazed at her reflection in the bathroom mirror and then glanced at the clock. Yikes! Late as usual.

She grabbed a sparkly clip and snapped it in her hair. She raced out of the apartment and down the spiral staircase that led to her family's restaurant in New York's Greenwich Village, the Waverly Sub Station. As she rushed down the stairs she almost crashed into her two brothers, Justin and Max, who were right in front of her. They were running late, too.

When the three Russo kids rushed into the kitchen, their mother was there waiting for them. She had packed up their lunches—courtesy of their sandwich shop—in brown paper bags.

"Oh," Mrs. Russo said, noticing Alex's short-sleeved shirt. "You might want to put on a jacket because it's very chilly outside."

Alex rolled her eyes. Her mother could be a little *too* protective sometimes! The weather wasn't that cold. But she knew her mom would not let up. "Fine. Stop all the racket, I'll wear a jacket." She smiled at her rhyme. Then she snapped her fingers, and a cute white jean jacket magically appeared over her shoulders.

"Hey!" Mr. Russo exclaimed, hurrying out from behind the sandwich-shop counter.

"Hey!" Alex greeted her dad.

4

"No, not 'hey.' I meant, '*Hey*!'" He sounded frustrated. "When your mom said to put on a jacket, she meant go get one, not pop one on."

"What's the big deal? It's just a jacket." Alex didn't know why her dad was so irritated. It wasn't as if he didn't know she was a wizard. Justin and Max were wizards, too. And Mr. Russo *used* to be one, but he gave up his powers when he married his wife, a nonwizard.

But only one of the Russo kids would actually be able to keep his or her magical powers once they turned eighteen. Until then they would try to learn as much magic as possible. Of course, no one was ever supposed to find out that they were wizards. The only person that knew was Alex's best friend Harper Evans, and she was sworn to secrecy. But the restaurant was empty.

"The big deal is, today it's just a jacket. But how long is it going to be before you're

5

popping a calculator into a math test?" her mom demanded.

"First it's cheating on math, then it's cheating on everything," her dad said sternly. "Then this happens, then that happens . . . then you're in jail," he concluded, his face grim.

"This happens and *that* happens?" Alex asked incredulously. Her parents could be so dramatic! "I just didn't want to walk upstairs."

"Well, walk upstairs, take that jacket off, then come back down and put it back on," her dad instructed.

Alex sighed. There would be no winning this one. "Anything to keep me out of jail," she muttered and trudged back up the stairs.

"Hey, Max, what's in the box?" Mrs. Russo asked her youngest son. She walked over to a table and inspected a plain shoe box that was sitting next to Max's backpack.

"Oh, it's my Mars diorama for school," he said proudly.

Mrs. Russo reached into the box and scooped up a handful of sand. "Where's the 'Mars' part?" she asked. She laughed as the sand fell through her fingers. "It's just a bunch of beach sand."

"Well, it's a pretty"—Max pulled out the teacher's instruction sheet and quickly read it over—"barren planet."

"What does 'barren' mean?" Justin challenged. Justin loved words. In fact, he loved anything to do with school. Of course, it was easy to love school when you were one of the smartest kids in your class!

Max glanced at his project. "Sandy?" he said hopefully.

Mrs. Russo sighed. "We'll discuss this later. You need to work harder, young man."

"Come on." Justin grabbed his brother's diorama. "Let's get your sandbox to school before a cat finds it."

Max groaned as he followed Justin out the

door. Last night, he'd thought he'd done a decent job. Now he realized his Mars shoe box looked more like a litter box. He sure hoped his teacher had a good imagination!

Alex bounded down the stairs for the second time that morning. "You see? Now I'm late." She pointed to the clock. "Can you at least write me a note?" she asked her dad.

"Sure," Mr. Russo said reluctantly. He pulled out his order pad and a pencil.

"Okay." Alex thought for a second, then began to dictate. "Dear Principal, Alex is late because her dad is a meanie for not letting her use magic to zap a jacket on." She looked up at her dad. He wasn't smiling. *Or* writing. "Okay, I'll run to school," Alex decided. She grabbed her messenger bag and dashed out the door.

She was barely down the block when she spotted a classmate of hers across the street. He was struggling to carry a huge binder.

"Hey, there's T. J.," she said aloud to herself.

T. J. Taylor was a student at Tribeca Prep, too.

As she was wondering whether to go up to him and say hello, he suddenly tripped on a crack in the sidewalk. He pitched forward, and the binder flew out of his arms. Alex started to cover her eyes so she wouldn't have to watch, but then time seemed to stand still. T. J. hovered midfall, both he and his binder floating in the air. Alex gasped as the binder turned and flew back into T. J.'s arms and he magically stood up again. He glanced about nervously, then— *poof*!—disappeared.

"Hey. Are you a—you just—wha—" Alex was so shocked that she couldn't form words. Did she really just see what she thought she'd seen? Definitely, she decided. "Look, wizard!" she managed to cry out.

She had just found another teenage wizard—and he went to her school!

Chapter Two

T. J. walked down the hall of Tribeca Prep. He hated high school. He was different from the other kids, and they never let him forget it. If they only knew I was a wizard, he thought, smiling to himself. Then I'd be the most popular guy around.

Suddenly, he bumped right into one of the huge players from the school's football team. The guy stood with a bunch of his friends, who were also very large. Uh-oh, T. J. thought.

He knew this meant trouble.

"Excuse *you*," the guy sneered. "Hey, guys, that kid's face reminded me. Want to get some pizza?"

The rest of the group snickered.

"I'll show you a pizza," T. J. retorted.

"What'd you say, kid?" the guy challenged, stepping closer.

T. J. gulped. "I said, 'I'll show you a pizza.'" Though it was T. J.'s only comeback, it never got old—or so he thought.

"You're always doing that. That doesn't even make sense." The guy turned to his friends and laughed.

"I'll show you what doesn't make sense," T. J. said. He hoped this guy wouldn't pound him.

"Dude, get a new insult book." The guy grinned at his comeback.

"I'll show you a new—" T. J. didn't get to finish his sentence. The guy grabbed the tube of yogurt that T. J. was holding and squirted it all over T. J.'s shirt.

The jock's friends doubled over in laughter. T. J. felt his face turn red. The guys high-fived each other, then strutted toward their next class.

T. J. waited until the hallway was empty. He hurried over to his locker. He turned the dial and glanced around again. All clear.

Or so he thought. What he didn't notice was Alex watching from around the corner.

He pointed his finger and a spark of white light flashed. Then a mini clothing rack emerged from his locker. The revolving rack turned, displaying a variety of miniaturized shirts and sweaters. T. J. regarded his choices. He pulled a brown sweater off the rack. With a snap of his fingers, the sweater became full-size and magically replaced the shirt he was wearing!

T. J. looked down at the sweater he now wore and, satisfied, again pointed his finger toward his locker. The clothing rack retreated inside and T. J.'s binder flew into his arms.

"Hey. Nice shirt," Alex said brightly, coming up behind him.

T. J. was shocked to see her standing there. "I'll show you a—" he began.

"Save it," Alex told him. She was on a mission. "So, um, your shirt appeared on your body as if by magic," she said, seeing if he would take the bait.

T. J. bit his lip. "Yeah, I change fast," he said nervously. "You know, I'm a quick-change artist. I was, uh, thinking of doing it for the talent show." He hoped she was buying his story.

Alex crossed her arms. "You're a wizard," she said simply.

"You mean with tools? Like the ones I used to build the clothes rack?" T. J.'s brain was spinning. He tried to think fast. "Yeah, I'm, uh, kind of a wizard."

Oh, please! Alex thought. "No, a wizard as in potions and brooms and spells," she said pointedly.

"Come on. A *wizard*?" T. J. forced out a chuckle, trying to play innocent.

"Hmm." Alex could see T. J. was not going to confess to being a wizard so easily. She shrugged casually. "Okay, I guess I was wrong. See you around." She started to walk away from him. But as she did, she intentionally shoved him with her shoulder, and his binder clattered to the floor.

Alex pretended to be surprised. "Sorry, I'm a klutz," she said and continued walking past him.

T. J. watched her go. Once she was out of sight, he snapped his fingers. His binder zoomed through the air and back over to him.

"Ha! I saw that!" Alex cried, jumping out from around the corner.

"Okay." T. J. tried to think of something to

say. But there really wasn't anything he could do now. "I'm a wizard," he confessed. "Don't tell anybody."

Alex smiled smugly. "It's okay. Because guess what? I'm a wizard, too."

T. J. raised his eyebrows. "You are? Prove it."

"Okay." She put her right hand behind her. "How many fingers am I holding behind my back?"

"How is this going to prove anything?" T. J. asked.

"Just guess," Alex said.

T. J. shrugged. "Four."

Alex grinned. "None. It's my foot." She pulled her arm in front of her—and instead of her hand, a foot was attached to the end!

T. J. nodded. "Oh, nice. The 'Feet for Hands' spell. I totally forgot about that one! Show me how it works."

"I can't. My parents are really strict about magic. I could get into so much trouble for doing that," Alex explained.

"Oh, that's lame," T. J. said as they started to walk down the hall together. "As long as nobody knows I'm a wizard, my parents let me use magic whenever I want."

"You're *so* lucky. I can't even magically switch jackets without my dad threatening to send me to jail," Alex complained.

"I don't know how you survive in this world," T. J. said, shaking his head.

"It's so hard being me," Alex agreed. She scratched her head with the foot that was still attached to her hand, then headed to her English class.

After school, T. J. was waiting for her by the main doors.

"Are you hungry?" he asked as they walked home together.

"Starving," Alex said.

T. J. stopped walking and snapped his fingers. All the people and cars around them froze. Then he pointed to a hot-dog cart across the street. Using the index fingers on both his right and left hands to direct his magic, he lifted two hot dogs from the pot of steaming water on the cart. The hot dogs floated into waiting buns. He started to raise the hot dogs, then paused. "Mustard or ketchup?" he asked Alex.

"The works," she told him. She couldn't believe they were using magic in plain view!

Alex watched as T. J. magically guided the ketchup and mustard bottles. They squirted the hot dogs. Then he guided the hot dogs through the air and into their hands.

Alex wrinkled her nose. "Aren't you going to pay for those?"

"Oh, right." T. J. snapped his fingers and a five dollar bill magically dropped onto the cart.

"Wow. Your life is so much easier than

mine," Alex said, taking a bite. Magic all the time is definitely the way to go, she thought.

A few minutes later, Alex entered the bustling Waverly Sub Station. Her family's restaurant was always busy in the afternoons. She spotted Justin and Max doing their homework at one of the front tables. She made her way over to them and nudged Justin.

"Hey," Justin said, and then he turned back to his study guide.

Alex gave her older brother another nudge.

"I said '*hey*,'" Justin repeated.

Alex rolled her eyes. She had to talk to Justin—this was important! She pulled him up by his shirt. "Will you get in here?" she said, heading toward the restaurant's kitchen.

Still confused, Justin followed his sister.

"Okay," Alex began when Justin was finally standing in front of her, "so I met an interesting guy at school today."

Justin groaned. "For the last time, I will

make my own friends, thank you!" Justin was sick of his sister's charity work—he thought his friends were just fine!

"Look," Alex said, exasperated, "you are making it so hard to be excited about something." She had big news to tell him! "This guy is a wizard, like us."

"Really? A kid from our school?" Justin's eyes lit up. "Oh, that is *so* cool! What's his name? Does he seem nice? We should totally have him over." He was practically jumping up and down with excitement.

"See, this is how you're going to ruin it." Alex reached out to steady him. "Just listen. It's T. J. Taylor."

Justin gasped. "T. J. Taylor's a *wizard*? Then that magic act he did at the school talent show was fake. I mean real. Which is what made it fake." Then Justin's eyes narrowed. "Oh, he needs to return that first-place ribbon. I'm making a call," he said, heading for the kitchen.

Alex grabbed him by the shirt again. "Justin, forget about the ribbon!" It was so like her brother to completely miss the big picture. "So you know that his parents let him use magic whenever he wants? Just think about how our lives would be."

Justin paused, thinking. "I could read books in the dark," he said dreamily.

Alex shook her head in disbelief. Could Justin be any more of a geek? She doubted it. "Magic is a waste with you. Besides using magic for what *electricity* can do, we need to get Dad to let us use magic whenever we want."

"Don't you already do that?" Justin pointed out.

"Yes," Alex said. "But I'm tired of getting in trouble for it. So, I'm going to tell Dad about T. J., and maybe that will get him to loosen up on the rules."

"But I love the rules!" Justin protested.

"Remember that summer when Dad said I could go to bed whenever I wanted?" He shuddered at the memory. "Oh, I was a mess."

"Well, rules bore me," Alex said. Already a plan was forming in her mind. "I'm going to talk to Dad when he's his happiest—after dinner and *before* pro wrestling."

It was simple! She would use logic to persuade her dad to let her do magic.

She was already imagining the endless possibilities of the magic-filled life ahead of her; that is, if she could convince her dad! She smiled to herself as she walked out of the kitchen. What could possibly go wrong?

Chapter Three

Alex scooted closer to her father on the sofa in their family room. She had just asked if she could use magic all the time, and her dad hadn't given her an answer yet. She was watching her dad nervously as he propped his feet up on the coffee table and reached for the remote control. Alex didn't know if she could take the agony any longer.

"Magic whenever you want . . ." Mr. Russo

finally said. He seemed to actually be considering it.

Please . . . Please . . . Alex begged silently.

"Hmm," her dad said. "No." Satisfied, he turned the TV on.

But Alex quickly grabbed the remote and turned the TV off. She wasn't done trying to convince him just yet. "But, Daddy, T. J.'s parents let him use magic all the time to do whatever. It's not fair," she pleaded. The everyone-else's-parents argument was definitely overused, but maybe this time it would work.

"Well, T. J. Taylor's parents aren't *your* parents," her dad said, taking the remote back from his daughter and turning the television back on. He tossed the remote onto the table, out of Alex's reach. "My house, my rules. Get your own house, you can make your own rules," he said matter-of-factly.

Alex sighed and stood up. "Fine," she

replied. She began to reach for her magic wand.

But her dad knew what she was up to. "And that's *not* me giving you permission to conjure up your own house," he warned.

She hung her head in defeat. "Shoot."

"Dad, do most Martians wear tinfoil or catcher's equipment?" Max asked, walking into the room with a green Martian mask pulled over his face. He was carrying a roll of aluminum foil in one hand and his catcher's mitt in the other.

Mr. Russo stared at his youngest son in amazement. "And you want me to add free-wheeling magic to this chaos?" he asked Alex. There was enough to handle even when the situation *didn't* involve magic!

"Hey, you guys!" Mrs. Russo called, running down the stairs and into the family room. "We're five minutes away from pro wrestling." She plopped herself down next to her husband on the sofa.

"Honey," Mr. Russo said to his wife, "Alex ran into another wizard at school, and now she's talking all kinds of nonsense like"—he began speaking in a very high-pitched version of Alex's voice—"*Oh, I want to do magic whenever I feel like.*"

"I don't talk like that!" Alex protested.

"There's another wizard family?" Mrs. Russo said, jumping up from the couch. "Because, you know, I would love to meet the parents and compare notes."

Alex was about to interrupt her mother when an idea popped into her head. If the two families got together maybe, just *maybe*, Alex could get her dad to change his mind!

At school the next afternoon, Alex and Justin cornered T. J. by the stairs. Alex was trying to convince T. J. to bring his parents over for dinner.

"I want to make sure your parents convince

my parents that everyday magic is okay, rather than the other way around," Alex told T. J. She had been up all night plotting to make sure the meeting didn't backfire on her.

"Oh, you don't have to worry about that," T. J. said casually.

Justin looked doubtful. "You don't know our dad. He'll throw a tantrum," he explained.

T. J. seemed unimpressed. "Who cares?" he said, and then paused. "All right, okay. A couple of years ago, I got into trouble for using magic. My parents tried to send me off to military school, so I put a charm on them so that no matter what I do, they go along with it. I mean, they're not even like parents, they're more like . . . my little robots."

"You *charmed* your parents?" Justin asked in disbelief.

Alex looked at T.J. in awe. She was impressed!

T. J. smiled. "Okay, so it's set. I'll clear my

parents' schedule, and we'll all come over for dinner tonight."

"Great," Alex said excitedly.

T. J. snapped his fingers. A spark of white light shot out. "There. They're free."

Justin's eyes widened in amazement. "You didn't even use a spell," he said, shocked.

"Oh, right. See, spells are like training wheels. When you're really good, you don't need them," T. J. said, smiling confidently.

Alex turned and walked to class. She had a good feeling about tonight!

Chapter Four

Back at the Russo home later that day, Max dropped a piece of paper into his mother's outstretched hand. He watched her face as she studied it.

"This is your Mars project?" she asked in confusion.

"Yep," Max said with a wide grin.

She peered closer at the photo on the paper. It was a picture of seven kids and one green-faced "Martian" in jeans and a sweatshirt, riding a roller coaster. A sign over the roller coaster read TRIP TO MARS. "That's not a Martian. That's *you* in a Martian mask," Mrs. Russo pointed out.

"How do you know that's me?" Max challenged. "That could be a real Martian, and I just happened to catch a photo of him conducting Earth-gravity experiments."

"On a ride called 'Trip to Mars'?" she asked.

"Yep," said Max.

"Hey! Look what I found in a plastic bag upstairs!" Mr. Russo exclaimed, rushing into the kitchen. "My old bowling shirt!" He lovingly smoothed out the red and blue polyester shirt that he was now wearing. "I thought you threw this out," he said to Mrs. Russo.

"Jerry, when you find something in a bag with used floss and empty shampoo bottles, it *was* thrown out," she replied, rolling her eyes. Then she turned to check on the dinner that was cooking in the oven. Alex began to set the table in preparation for what could be a life-changing night for her and her brothers. Her parents had agreed to have T.J. and his parents over for dinner that night. Alex couldn't wait for her family to meet another family of wizards!

"Honey, I want you to put something nice on for the Taylors," Mrs. Russo told her husband.

But Mr. Russo shook his head. "It doesn't matter what I wear when I tell them what they are doing wrong with their kid," he informed his wife.

"Ding-dong!" three voices suddenly sang out from the living room.

The Russos entered the room and gasped. T. J. had suddenly appeared with his dad, a tall dark-haired man in a button-down shirt, and his mom, a woman with short blond hair. The three Taylors smiled as if it were completely natural to *beam* yourself into someone's family room.

"Oh, so the freewheeling magic starts now," Mr. Russo muttered. He eyed the Taylor family suspiciously.

"Look! They *popped* in!" Mrs. Russo tried her best to sound delighted. She quickly smoothed her hair and hoped the apartment looked clean enough.

Alex hurried over to her parents. "That's right," she said. "No one had to get the door. What's more courteous than magic?" she pointed out, trying to put a positive spin on it. "Nothing!"

"I'm Theresa, and this is my husband, Jerry," Alex's mom said, smiling and reaching out to shake hands with T. J.'s parents.

"This is my wife, Lori," Mr. Taylor said.

"I brought you a noodle kugel." Mrs. Taylor smiled brightly and thrust a covered dish into Mrs. Russo's hands.

"Oh, thank you!" Mrs. Russo exclaimed.

"Hey," T. J. said, turning to Alex.

Alex grabbed him and pulled him toward the spiral staircase just as Justin bounded down the last few steps.

"Uh, T. J.," Alex said, glancing nervously to see if her dad was watching her. But he was too busy talking with T. J.'s father. "Justin and I would love to show you the lair. Come on." The Wizard's Lair was a special room in the basement where Mr. Russo gave Alex, Justin, and Max their magic lessons.

"Okay," T. J. said, shrugging.

"No, I wouldn't," Justin said. "I'm staying here to watch your plan blow up." He smiled smugly at Alex. "Metaphor," he explained. Justin took any chance he could to prove he was the smartest one in the family.

"Well, *I'll* be the one laughing like a hyena," Alex replied.

"Simile," Justin sneered.

"No," Alex said. "Animal joke." She smirked and turned to go.

But as she was leaving with T. J., she noticed that her dad was watching them. Time to put her plan into action. "Oh, *no*," she said to T. J., but loud enough for all the adults to hear. "It's kind of chilly down there. And you don't have a jacket. If only you could *zap* yourself a jacket."

"I can take care of this, no problem," T. J. announced. He snapped his fingers. But instead of zapping a jacket onto himself, a wood-burning stove appeared in front of him. T. J. warmed his hands over the crackling fire. "Mmm. Toasty."

"Oh, look, honey. There's a wood-burning stove in the middle of our loft. There's nothing strange about that," Mr. Russo said sarcastically.

Alex decided to ignore her dad's tone of voice. She and T. J. needed to figure out the best way to convince Mr. Russo that using magic all the time was a great idea. She turned and headed down the hall to the lair door, T. J. following behind her. The wood-burning stove started to follow them, too!

"Oh, look! It's moving." Mr. Russo pointed to the stove and Mrs. Russo laughed nervously. "Hey! Not too close to the shelves," Mr. Russo called after Alex. The stove was practically knocking things over as it moved down the hallway. "We need those books, so we don't look like we watch too much TV."

Alex sighed. Her plan had *not* gotten off to a very good start. She led T. J. down the stairs to the lair. The room was filled with old spell books, vials of potions, wands, and other cool wizard tools. "Here's our lair," she said.

T. J. looked around. He seemed unimpressed. "My whole house is full of magic stuff," T. J. bragged. "I mean, there's this one room, you open the door, it's a black hole. I know. Cool, right?"

"Your life is so great! I just hope your parents convince my parents that we can use magic with no rules," Alex said wistfully.

"You don't have to worry about that," T. J. assured her.

Alex shook her head. T. J. obviously didn't know what he was up against. "My dad can be pretty stubborn."

"Not after he eats the kugel, he won't be." T. J. smiled mysteriously.

"Well, what does that have to do with my dad?" Alex asked.

"Oh, the charm I put on my mom and dad, it's in the kugel. It's what gives it the cinnamon-y flavor," T. J. said matter-of-factly.

"So wait," said Max, who had been sitting in another corner of the room, listening to their conversation. "When our parents eat it, they're going to be under the spell, too?"

T. J. nodded, and Max reached over the side of the sofa to give him a high five.

"You're welcome," T. J. said, slapping palms with Max.

"This is great!" Alex exclaimed. She couldn't believe how easy this was going to be. "The only thing that could possibly make this better is if Justin were here to hate it."

Max laughed.

Meanwhile, the four adults and Justin had gathered in the family room, and were sitting with plates of kugel on their laps.

Mr. Russo got right to the point. "Don't you think it's a little irresponsible to let T. J. use magic whenever he wants?" he asked Mr. and Mrs. Taylor as he took a forkful of kugel. "Mmm. Cinnamon-y."

"Yes, it is completely irresponsible," Mr. Taylor agreed, nodding. But he didn't seem to care. He had a happy, vacant look in his eyes.

"What? I thought it was okay for him to use magic," Justin interrupted.

"It is absolutely okay for T. J. to use magic," Mr. Taylor said. Justin looked at his dad for a reaction.

"That is so right." Mr. Russo agreed as he took another large bite of kugel. "You know, I like your parenting style, Taylor." He smiled at T. J.'s father.

Justin gaped at his dad. What was he saying? Had he lost his mind?

"What do you think, honey?" Mr. Russo asked his wife.

"Mmm." Mrs. Russo licked her lips. "The only thing I like better than freewheeling magic is this kugel!" she exclaimed.

"*What?*" Justin cried. "Dad, you hate magic without rules," he said to his father.

"Relax. Have some kugel," Mrs. Russo told her son.

"I'm allergic to cinnamon. That's why I get my own pie at Thanksgiving," Justin reminded her.

"Ooh, yeah. The bland pie." Mrs. Russo giggled.

Justin looked at his parents in shock. What was going on?

Suddenly, Alex, Max, and T. J. came up from the lair and wandered into the room. "Oh, so I see you enjoyed the kugel," Alex said, a sly grin on her face.

"Oh, kugel!" Max's eyes lit up and he lunged for the casserole dish.

"Max!" Alex grabbed him by the back of his shirt. Had he completely forgotten what T. J. had just told them about the kugel?

"Alex, I don't believe it," Justin said, pulling her aside. "Your misguided plan actually worked! The Taylors convinced Mom and Dad to let us use magic whenever we want."

Alex smiled. "And now you can read in the dark all you want."

Justin nodded. "I'm happy about that, but a little bit guilty . . ." he admitted. He couldn't believe his parents had agreed so fast. "And also suspicious . . ." he continued. Taking a breath, he inhaled the aroma from the kugel. "And a little bit hungry."

Alex patted her brother on the back and tossed him an apple from a bowl on the counter. She stared at her parents and the Taylors chatting happily like old friends. Mission accomplished!

Now it was time to put these magic powers to work!

Chapter Five

The next morning, Alex entered the Waverly Sub Station wearing a plain sweatshirt and jeans—very unusual considering the more fashionable outfits she usually wore.

"Hey Mom, I don't know what to wear," she complained.

"Oh. Well, what are you thinking?" Mrs. Russo asked.

Alex smiled mischievously. Choosing clothes usually took a long time for her. The process required multiple outfit changes and always resulted in piles of rejected clean clothes heaped onto her bedroom floor. But it wasn't going to take long this time!

"Well, I'm thinking instead of trying on a bunch of stuff and showing you, it would just be easier to do this." Alex pointed her wand toward the center of the empty restaurant. A white light flashed. Then a long, brightly lit catwalk appeared.

Mrs. Russo gasped. The Waverly Sub Station now looked like the set of a real, live fashion show!

"Is that okay?" Alex asked hesitantly, and held her breath.

"If it's okay with you, it's okay with me," Mrs. Russo said, smiling calmly.

"Just making sure," Alex said and exhaled. "Thank you, kugel," she said under her breath.

"Ooh, I love that kugel," her mom said dreamily, overhearing what Alex had just said.

Suddenly, hip-hop music started blaring through the loudspeakers as models began to strut down the catwalk. Each model looked exactly like Alex, and each wore a different funky outfit.

"Okay, so I like the shoes on this one," Alex said pointing to the first model, "but the shirt's too light, and the hat's cute on this one. . . ." She nodded at the third model.

"Well, I think—" her mom began.

"Ooh, *that's* the one!" Alex exclaimed as a model wearing the cutest outfit appeared. She pointed her wand toward the model, and suddenly Alex was wearing the same outfit! "Thank you, Mom!" she exclaimed, delighted.

Mrs. Russo smiled. "You're welcome, sweetie."

Mr. Russo walked out from the kitchen. "Ooh, a catwalk," he said excitedly, when he noticed the runway. He ran over and leaped up on it. He sashayed down the platform as if he, too, were a model.

"Oh, this is awkward," Alex groaned. It was time to get to school, before her Dad did anything more embarrassing. She waved her wand.

A split second later, she was standing in front of her locker. She opened her combination lock and pulled a notebook from the shelf. Then her stomach growled. "Oh, shoot. I'm hungry. I forgot to eat breakfast," she said to herself.

She was going to head to the cafeteria, but she quickly realized that her hunger pangs could be easily fixed with magic. "*Comemakeus Pancakeus*," she chanted. Then she reached into her locker and pulled out a plate stacked high with fluffy pancakes drizzled with maple syrup. "Mmm."

Suddenly, Justin ran through the main doors and over to Alex. He was completely out of breath. "Oh, phew. I made it! I missed the subway."

"Well, why didn't you use magic to transport

yourself here?" Alex asked him. "Have you used *any* magic since the rules were lifted?"

"*Yes*," Justin said defensively.

Alex rolled her eyes. "Besides reading in the dark?" she asked.

"Then, no, I haven't had time," Justin admitted. "I overslept, so I was late."

"That's the perfect time to use it!" Alex exclaimed. Justin was totally missing out on all the fun. "You're afraid, aren't you?" she asked. She knew her brother too well.

"No!" Justin exclaimed, still being defensive.

"Prove it," Alex challenged. "Use magic right now."

Justin looked over at Alex and nodded. He walked down the hall to his locker. Alex shut hers and followed. Justin twirled his combination dial back and forth. Then he opened the locker door.

"That's not magic," Alex complained.

"How do you know I didn't forget my

locker combination and then used magic to remember it?" Justin replied.

"Because you made up a locker-combination song." Alex began to sing, *"Right to clear it, come on let's hear it. Twenty-three . . ."*

Justin joined in and they finished the song together: *"Left eight digits, but don't fidget. Thirty-one. Now for the last, don't go too fast. Six, and you're off to class. Boo!"*

When the song was over, Alex hurried off to her math class. She arrived and sat at her desk, her notebook open and a pencil ready, but she wasn't paying attention to anything her teacher was saying. She was too busy day-dreaming about all of the wonderful ways she could use magic. She wished she could convince Justin to at least try a spell or two.

It wasn't until after school that the perfect magical opportunity presented itself.

"Miss Weston didn't like my 'Aliens on a

Roller Coaster' project," Max complained to Alex and Justin. The three of them were doing homework together at a table in the Waverly Sub Station. "She is so obsessed with this Mars thing," Max continued.

"Perfect," Alex said, a sly grin spreading across her face. "Justin, I'm going to show you how to enjoy using magic in a way you'll understand. You're going to help Max with his Mars project. *Transportium*—"

"Oh, no," Justin interrupted Alex's spell. "There is no way I'm actually going to the surface of—"

"*Nextorbitorium*." Alex completed the spell before Justin could complete his sentence.

"Mars." Justin finally finished his thought as he looked around. They were exactly where he didn't want to be—standing on Mars! Justin started gasping for air but then realized that they could *magically* breathe in outer space.

"It's all sand!" Max exclaimed, looking at the miles of reddish sand and rock. "My shoe box looked just like this."

"This is dangerous, Alex. We shouldn't be here," Justin warned.

"Hey, look!" Max pointed to something nearby in the sand. "The Mars Rover!" Nearby was the infamous, robotic car!

Justin's eyebrows shot up. "No, *not* cool. Don't break it!" he shouted to Max, who was heading right for it. The rover was a machine that had been sent up to Mars years ago, and it was controlled by computers on Earth. It sent back all sorts of information about Mars.

Suddenly, the rover lit up and began to beep.

"This doesn't look right," Max said uneasily. But then he decided to ignore the beeping metal machine. He picked up a handful of smooth stones that had been retrieved by the rover. "These rocks will be great for my report."

"No, no, no." Justin reached to grab the stones. "Max, come on. We're going. You can't upset the natural order of things."

"What are you talking about?" Alex demanded. She was still stunned that she had actually transported them all the way to Mars!

"If we can't take rocks from Yosemite, I'm pretty sure we can't take them from Mars," Justin explained. Last summer their family had visited the famous national park in California. There had been signs all over warning them to leave the natural resources alone.

"What is your problem?" Alex asked. Justin always took the fun out of their adventures.

"I can hardly believe Mom and Dad would be okay with this," Justin said.

Alex sighed. "Of *course* they're okay with it. Just like T. J.'s parents are. That's what *charming* your parents means."

Justin gasped. "Mom and Dad are *charmed*?" he cried. "What? How? When? Who?"

"Mom and Dad," Alex said calmly, answering Justin's last question.

"What? How? When?" Justin sputtered.

"At dinner," Alex told him.

"How?" Justin continued.

"It was in the kugel," Alex explained.

"*What?*" he asked again.

"Justin, I think you *know* what," Alex said, exasperated.

Suddenly, it all made sense. His parents. The magic. The kugel. Justin groaned. "We have to fix this!" he yelled.

"It's already fixed," Alex said. "We can use magic whenever we want."

"But that's what I'm trying to fix!" Justin threw his arms up in frustration.

"That's not fixing anything," Alex quipped.

"*Transportium nextorbitorium*," Justin began to chant.

Suddenly, a bright white light flashed. Justin and Alex felt themselves being sucked into a giant wind tunnel. They sped through the air at a dizzying pace, cold wind whipping against their faces.

Then they were back in their apartment, in their own kitchen.

"Mom!" Justin cried, out of breath. "You're charmed!"

Mrs. Russo glanced up from chopping vegetables. She smiled at her eldest son. "Yes, I am. Thank you, honey."

"You don't mind?" Justin asked, still confused.

Alex gave her clueless brother a shove. "Of course she doesn't mind," she said.

Mrs. Russo smiled vacantly. "I don't mind anything. Not even that there's a big piece of space junk in my living room." She pointed to the small robotic car parked next to the sofa.

Mr. Russo hurried over from the stove. "Ooh! Is that the solar-powered toaster I've always dreamed of?"

Justin clenched his teeth. "No, it's the Mars Rover. And guess what it's *not* doing: roving Mars!" He couldn't believe the machine was in their living room. It must have gotten mixed up in his spell somehow!

"Ooh, the Mars Rover." Mr. Russo rubbed his hands together in delight and chuckled. "That'll be great for Max's project."

Justin and Alex looked at each other in horror.

"Max!" they screamed in unison.

"Oh, my goodness!" Alex cried. "We left Max on Mars!"

Chapter Six

Meanwhile, back on Mars, Max peered around another pile of reddish sand. There was nothing in sight for miles, except for some red rocks and lots of sand. Boy, this planet really *is* barren, he thought.

And it was oddly quiet, too.

Max couldn't hear Justin or Alex, and they were pretty loud when they argued—which was most of the time. Max looked around. Nothing. No one.

Suddenly, Max had a horrible sinking feeling in his stomach. He was all alone.

"Guys? Guys?" he called. Where were Alex and Justin? He stood right where they had landed after the spell back on Earth was spoken. He could even see his brother's and sister's footprints in the sand. Then he noticed that the Mars Rover was missing, too. "They ditched me." He shook his head in disbelief. Why did this always happen to him?

His stomach growled. All he wanted was to be back home, where he could raid the fridge. "What's that spell again?" he asked himself. He would try his best to do magic and fix things.

"*Comemakeus Pancakeus*," he chanted, and a large stack of pancakes, dripping with butter and syrup, suddenly appeared. "I remembered!" Max was pleased with himself. He sat down on a nearby rock to eat . . . and wait.

Back in the Russo home, Alex and Justin were panicking. "Max is on Mars," Alex repeated to her parents, waiting for their reaction to the news.

"Ooh, isn't that nice?" her mom replied casually. She was totally in another world!

"No, you don't understand. I left Max on Mars." Alex waited. Her mother and father continued to smile. It was eerie. "I should be in big trouble right now, and Dad should be fixing it," Alex wailed. She hoped Max was okay.

"What's to fix? Max will be fine," Mr. Russo said, shrugging his shoulders. "Just use the spell you used to go to Mars to get him back."

"You mean you don't even care that we left our brother on Mars?!" Alex cried. What was with her parents? When were they going to snap out of it?

"We're just happy you're all having fun with magic," her dad replied. He grinned again.

"It's not about that." Alex wanted to shake some sense into them. "It's about you not caring, and on top of this, I'm disrupting a million dollar space program!"

"*Billion* dollar," Justin corrected her.

"Billion dollar?" Alex was totally panicking. She turned to her dad. "*Billion* dollar space program! And I'm scared."

"Scared's good," her dad said casually.

"No, it's not!" Alex protested. "It's dangerous."

"Dangerous is good," her dad said.

"No, it's not. That's why we have rules," Alex reminded her father. "So we don't do anything that's scary or dangerous." She couldn't believe what she was saying—but it was all true!

"Are you saying that you want rules?" Her mother sounded confused.

"Yes, I want rules! And, more importantly, I want my parents back." Alex was freaked out. This was the time when the adults were supposed to jump in and fix all the stuff she had majorly messed up. "Snap out of it. You're under a spell."

"Oh, isn't that nice? She put a spell on us." Her mom laughed giddily. Mr. Russo chuckled, too.

Alex was beside herself. What were they going to do?

"Okay," Justin said. It was time to take charge. "You take the rover back to Mars and get Max," he instructed Alex. "I'm going to figure out how to reverse the spell on Mom and Dad. To the thinking chamber!" He waved his arms dramatically.

Alex rolled her eyes. "You mean your bedroom," she said.

"Do you want me to help or not?" Justin asked.

"Sorry," Alex said. She knew she needed Justin now more than ever. "To your thinking chamber!"

She watched Justin hurry up the stairs. Then she took a deep breath. She hoped she could zap herself back to Mars. With her, magic was kind of unpredictable.

"*Transportium nextorbitorium*," she chanted.

After Alex had left, Justin had come up with a plan. Now he was standing by his parents, who were on the couch in the living room digging into a treat he had baked just for them. "You guys like the brownies?" Justin asked. He eyed his parents nervously as they both chewed.

"Delicious," Mr. Russo said through a mouthful of chocolate. He turned to his son. "Is there any more kugel left?"

"No!" Justin cried. He had to think of something more—and fast!

Suddenly, Alex magically appeared in the family room—with Max by her side! Justin breathed a sigh of relief. He couldn't believe that Alex had succeeded in bringing Max back from outer space!

"Oh, it's good to be home," Max said.

Alex sniffed. "Whoa. Brownies? This is what your thinking chamber came up with?" she asked Justin.

"It turns out the cocoa powder in the brownies reverses the spell," he explained.

"That's ridiculous," Alex scoffed.

"Wh—wh—why is there red dust all over my living room?" Mrs. Russo stammered and spun around, as if noticing her home and her children for the first time.

"It's . . ." Mr. Russo suddenly pointed to the little wheeled robot. His eyes grew wide. "There . . . Mars . . . *who* . . . Alex!"

"Maybe it's not *that* ridiculous," Alex said to Justin. Clearly the brownies had done *something*!

"Not to mention she left me on Mars," Max piped up.

Their parents gasped.

Alex stepped forward. "He's right. It's all my fault," she admitted.

"You are in so much trouble, young lady," her father warned.

Alex smiled sincerely. "I know." Her parents didn't sound like spaced-out pod people anymore. They sounded like her normal parents. And she couldn't have been happier.

Once Alex, Justin, and Max had explained everything to their parents, they wasted no time inviting Mr. and Mrs. Taylor back to their apartment.

"Here you go," Mrs. Russo said, ushering her guests in and showing them to the sofa. She handed each of them a brownie. "Alex and Justin were happy to make you these brownies."

Mrs. Taylor pushed it away. "T.J. says eating brownies is against the law."

"Um. That law was overturned yesterday.

It was in the, uh . . ." Mr. Russo glanced at the newspaper in his hand and quickly tossed it aside. "I mean, don't you read the papers?"

"Oh." Mr. Taylor nodded, easily convinced. He took a bite. "Mmm."

Mrs. Taylor also took a bite. Then another. "Delightful."

"Mm-hmm. Delicious!" Mr. Taylor agreed.

"Uh, where is T. J.?" Alex asked.

"Mmm. He's busy riding up the side of the Empire State Building on a skateboard," Mrs. Taylor said.

Suddenly, the front door burst open, and there was T. J., skateboard in hand. "I made it!" T. J. explained triumphantly. "I made it all the way to the—" He stopped suddenly, as he noticed his parents feasting on the dessert. "Brownies!" he cried.

"You're in trouble, young man." Mrs. Taylor stood up. Her eyes narrowed into a steely gaze.

Part 1

Alex's parents scolded her for using magic outside the lair. "What's the big deal?" she asked.

"I'm a wizard, too!" Alex exclaimed.

"Magic whenever you want? No,"
Mr. Russo told Alex.

Alex had successfully cast a spell on her parents
that let her practice magic whenever she wanted!

Alex transported herself and her brothers to Mars!

"You mean you don't even care that we left Max on Mars?" Alex asked her parents.

Justin hoped that the brownies he had
baked would reverse the spell.

Alex was so glad that her parents
were back to normal.

Part 2

Justin successfully turned a guinea pig into a dove during his wizard exam.

"Alex Russo, your exam results plus your homework equals an F," the magic report card announced.

Alex ripped up her report card,
hoping to get rid of it.

*"These parents are now not. Two guinea pigs
should fill their slot!"* Alex chanted.

Alex had turned her parents into guinea pigs. But then Max and Justin lost them!

Alex and Justin spotted their parents under Max's bed!

"Alex, do you want to tell Professor Crumbs where we were?" her father asked her.

"You make me a better wizard," Justin told Alex, giving her a hug.

T. J. glanced at Alex, but Alex just shrugged. She had certainly learned why following her parents' rules was important, and now it was T. J.'s turn. There'd be no more breakfast with a snap of her fingers, or zapping on clothes, but that was okay by Alex. For now, magic was going to be kept in the lair—where it belonged!

PART
TWO

Chapter One

Alex Russo chewed the end of her pencil, deep in thought. She stared at the wizard test sitting before her and debated about whether her last answer was right. She kind of doubted it. She always had trouble remembering the words to spells.

She casually turned her head ever-so-slightly to the left and tried to peek at her older brother Justin's paper. He was the book-smart one in this family, so a little peek could make a big difference in Alex's grade!

Justin covered his test with his arm and scowled at Alex. She stuck out her tongue. She had the urge to make some comment about Justin's nerdiness, but there was no talking during a test. Even a test about magic given by your dad in your family's secret basement lair.

Alex didn't bother turning the other way to check out her little brother Max's paper. He was pretty bad at all this wizard stuff, too.

"Okay, last question," Mr. Russo announced. He stood at the front of the lair, clipboard in hand. "Bat wings, dragon scales, and fruit punch make what kind of potion? A. Invisibility. B. Skin of steel. C. A refreshing fruit smoothie."

"Got it," Justin announced. He scribbled down his answer.

"Does he have to say 'got it' after every question?" Alex complained. "It's throwing me off on my exam."

Max gasped and dropped his pencil. "We're taking an exam?" He looked truly surprised. But, then again, lots of things surprised Max, who often lived in his own world.

Suddenly, a bell rang.

"Time!" their dad announced. "Pencils down."

Alex dropped her pencil. She didn't know the answer anyway.

"Last exam section. Grab your wands and line up," Mr. Russo instructed. He walked across the room to a table that held three cages. Inside each cage sat a guinea pig. "You have to use the transfiguration spell to change one of these guinea pigs into a white dove. Okay, Justin. You're up," Mr. Russo said, turning to his eldest son.

Justin approached the table. He raised his wand and chanted, *"This guinea pig is now not. A dove with wings should fill its slot."*

Suddenly, a green light flashed from the end

of Justin's wand. The guinea pig disappeared, and in its place appeared a white dove!

"Very good, Justin." Mr. Russo nodded his head, impressed. "Alex, you're up."

Alex walked slowly to the table. She pointed her wand at the second cage. "Oh, okay." She tried to concentrate. "*Um, this guinea pig is now not. A dove with wings should fill its slot,*" she chanted, trying to sound confident.

Just then, red, then orange, then purple light flashed from her wand. The Russos held their breath. And then . . . the guinea pig disappeared! Alex stared at its replacement. There was a brick in the cage. That's definitely not a bird, she thought. *So* not good. But she tried to play it off.

"Ooh, it's a pretty dove," Alex cooed, though she knew her dad wouldn't buy it.

Her dad sighed. "No." He pointed to the cage. "You weren't concentrating. Max, you're up."

Max stepped forward. He drew his wand

and chanted quickly, *"This guinea pig is now not. A dove with wings should fill with snot."*

His wand flashed a rainbow of colors. Then the guinea pig in the third cage was replaced by a dove—a *sneezing* dove.

Alex laughed. Max had fumbled his spell, too.

Max looked horrified. "I said *snot*, didn't I?"

Alex nodded.

"Okay, everybody, record your transfiguration result in your midterm exam text booklets," Mr. Russo instructed.

"I don't know why you guys even bother taking the tests," Justin told Alex and Max smugly. He plopped down in a velvet-covered chair nearby. "We all know that *I'm* the one that's going to win the family wizard contest and keep my powers."

"That's not for a long while, Justin," Alex said. She hated when her brother acted so superior. In every wizard family, only one person was allowed to keep his or her powers. The rules dictated that the best wizard kept them. And even though Justin and Alex were forced to compete in the competition early on vacation—or else their family would disappear forever—Justin always assumed he would beat out Alex and Max when the real time came.

"And what if they change the rules so only girls keep their powers?" Alex asked. She pretended to think about it. "Oh, wait, you still might win," she said snidely.

"Oh, Alex, you're so transparent," Justin said. "You know I'm better than you at magic, so you have to lash out and make fun of me." He turned to Max. "And you don't take any of this magic seriously."

Alex snorted. "I can't take *you* seriously! You use big words like transparent!" she exclaimed.

Suddenly a huge floor-to-ceiling glass

window in the lair swung open. A smoky haze filled the room, and an older man walked in wearing a long, flowing black robe and a small black hat. He had a scraggly white beard that reached to his knees.

"Professor Crumbs," Mr. Russo said, and nodded to the esteemed headmaster of Wiz Tech, the top school for wizards. "Always nice to see you," he said pleasantly.

"Jerry," Professor Crumbs greeted Mr. Russo. Then he turned to the Russo kids. "I'm here to collect your exams and take them back to Wiz Tech," he said.

Justin handed his paper to the headmaster. Alex reluctantly did the same.

"Why doesn't Dad just grade our papers?" Max asked as he handed over his exam.

"So that no one will get better grades just by batting their eyes and trying to look cute," the headmaster explained, giving Alex a pointed look.

Alex smiled and blinked a few times. Her innocent look was extremely well practiced. "Are you talking about me?" she asked sweetly.

Justin mimicked her motions and tone of voice. "Alex, you're doing it right now."

Professor Crumbs and Mr. Russo laughed.

Alex frowned. That wasn't the result she had hoped for. Now all she could do was hope that she had gotten some answers right on the test, because she definitely didn't have a backup plan. And that was *never* good.

Chapter Two

A few days later, Max rushed through the apartment door waving three large yellow envelopes. Each envelope had a shiny gold sticker on the front. He tossed his backpack on the floor and announced, "Wizard report cards are here!"

Alex glanced up from typing a text message to her best friend, Harper Evans. "Oh," she said, unimpressed. "*You* sound excited," she said to Max. "You must feel confident you did well."

"Oh," Max said and paused. Suddenly, reality hit him, and he changed his tone. "Wizard report cards are here," he repeated. This time he sounded nervous.

"You first," Alex said.

Max ripped open the envelope and slid out a large, folded card. He placed the card on the arm of the sofa. Suddenly, the sound of trumpets filled the family room. Then the card opened by itself and began to speak.

"Max Russo, your exam results plus your course work equals a solid C-plus," the report card announced.

Max pumped his fist in the air. "Sweet! I got a C," he said enthusiastically.

Alex reached for her envelope and ripped it open. She held the card in her palm. Again, trumpets blared.

"Alex Russo," her report card bellowed, "your exam results, plus the homework you handed in on greasy napkins, all equals"—Alex held her breath—"F. And the F is a *low* F."

Alex raised her eyebrows. "*Excuse* me?" she asked the card. "I turned a guinea pig into a very solid brick. Which, I think, is a *much* more effective symbol for peace."

"Please have your parents sign me so I can return to Wiz Tech and receive my payment. I have to make a living," her report card quipped.

Alex slammed the card shut. She couldn't have her parents find out about this. She stood up and headed for the kitchen. "Yeah, right. Like *that's* going to happen." She pushed the pedal on the garbage can, and the lid flipped open.

"No! No! No!" her report card cried. Alex tossed it in with the trash and slammed the lid closed.

Problem solved, she thought.

Max perched himself on a stool at the kitchen counter. "Uh, what are you going to do? Mom and Dad need to sign that."

Alex shrugged. "Well, they can't sign something that never got here."

"But it got here," Max said.

"No, it didn't," Alex replied.

"Yes, it did," Max protested.

"Yes, it did," Alex said, repeating what he had just said.

"No, it didn't," Max said, automatically taking the other side of the argument.

"What are we talking about?" Alex asked innocently.

Max stopped and tried to think. He was completely confused. "I don't know."

Alex smiled. "Perfect."

At that moment, Justin rushed through the front door and immediately spotted his Wiz Tech envelope on the coffee table. "Ooh, the report cards are here!" he exclaimed. He sat on the sofa, unzipped his backpack, and pulled out a gold frame and set it on the table. "I have to make a copy for my new frame!"

Justin tore open his envelope. He couldn't wait for the good news. He set the card on the table and listened to the trumpet fanfare.

"Justin Russo, your exam results plus your course work equals all As and one B-plus. You're the smart one," said his report card.

Justin's face fell. "B-*plus*?" He always got all As! He shook his head sadly. "I can't put this in a frame!"

Later that afternoon, Alex was feeling pretty pleased with herself. She'd definitely delayed her inevitable 'you've-got-to-study-harder' grounding. By the time her parents would come looking for her report card, she'd just say it got lost in the mail. Once they'd called Wiz Tech and tracked it down, at least two weeks would have passed. She could definitely come up with a plan—and have some fun—in two weeks.

In the empty kitchen of the Waverly Sub

Station, her family's restaurant, Alex tucked three slices of cheese between two pieces of bread. She liked her grilled cheese extra gooey. She opened the microwave door to pop in her sandwich. Suddenly her report card flew out!

"Ooh, I love it in there! It smells like popcorn," the report card said, settling on the counter.

"Why don't you *hush*?" Alex whispered to the piece of paper. She looked around worriedly, making sure she was truly alone. Then she narrowed her eyes at the report card. "I thought I threw you away."

"You can't throw me away. I need a parent to sign me. And preferably with a nice felt-tip pen," the card said.

"See you later, honey," Alex's father called from just outside the kitchen door. "I'll be back in an hour."

Alex panicked. What if he came in? She

grabbed the report card. Her eyes darted around the kitchen.

Where to hide it? Where to hide it? she wondered frantically. The refrigerator? The stove?

Quickly, she tossed it into a big sink filled with dirty dishes that were soaking in soapy water. She pushed the paper deep under the soap bubbles just as her dad came in.

"I'm going for a jog," he announced. He raised his eyebrows when he saw Alex's hands submerged in the dirty dishwater. "Are you doing the dishes?" he asked incredulously.

"Uh, yeah, sure." Alex smiled weakly and reached for a dish.

Her dad nodded. "Oh, *I* know what you are doing. You're afraid of what's going to happen when your report card gets here, so you're trying to be extra good." He laughed.

Alex laughed along with him. It was always good to let him think he'd outsmarted her.

"Yep. You always know what I'm up to, Dad," she said with a smile.

Mr. Russo grinned and jogged out the door.

As soon as he was gone, Alex shoved her report card down the garbage disposal. She flipped the switch and the motor whirred. Time for some shredding action!

"I'm back!" her report card suddenly called out. It sat on the counter across the kitchen in one piece, looking as if it had just arrived in the mail.

What? How? Alex's brain was spinning. She stared at the drain, and then back at her report card. What was going on here?

Her confusion quickly morphed into anger. "Oh, yeah? Let's see if you keep talking when you're full of hot sauce!" She grabbed a bottle of the fiery liquid and doused the card.

"Ow! Ow! That *is* hot!" it screamed.

But the report card was tougher than she'd imagined—it wasn't giving up! Alex headed upstairs to the Russos' apartment, with the report card clenched tightly in her hand. She needed to think. She needed to figure out how to get rid of this enchanted—and very annoying—card.

She walked through the family room and out the sliding glass door that led to their terrace.

"You know what? I feel bad for you," the card said. "I'm going to tell you how to get rid of a bad report card."

"Really? How?" Alex asked, suddenly very alert.

"Get good grades," the report card replied.

That was not the answer Alex had been looking for! She tore the card in half. Then she tore it again. And again.

"Alex, what are you doing?" Alex heard a voice ask her.

Alex spun around. Her mother was standing behind her. She was holding a tall glass of iced tea and a magazine.

"Mom!" Alex quickly tossed the pieces of paper over the side of the terrace. The tiny pieces fluttered down four stories to the ground. "That was just confetti, for the parade," she fibbed.

Mrs. Russo peered over the side of the wall. There were people on the sidewalks and a few cars and taxis on the street. "There's no parade," she commented, raising an eyebrow.

Alex tried to come up with a quick explanation. "Not yet. But there will be. And how proud are we going to be when we're the first ones to throw the confetti? My guess? Pretty proud," Alex said, wondering if she sounded at all believable.

Mrs. Russo stared at Alex in confusion. Then she glanced at a chaise lounge longingly. "You know what? I've got a magazine and an iced tea. I'm good with whatever you're up to," her mom told her. She walked over to the cushy chair and stretched out.

As she adjusted her sunglasses, a white piece

of paper slowly rose from the pages of the magazine that she held in her hand.

Alex gasped. Her report card! She lunged for the magazine, grabbing it from her mother's hand. "Hey! Is that the new issue of *Urban Terrace Gardening*?" She quickly opened the magazine. "I've been waiting for that."

"Alex!" her mother cried, sitting up straight.

Alex started to back away toward the doors that led back into the apartment, when all of a sudden, her dad burst through them!

"I got to the corner, and I realized I forgot to stretch. And it's hot!" he said, breathing heavily. He wiped the sweat dripping off his forehead. "I think I'll start jogging in the fall," he said.

The report card, meanwhile, began its trumpet fanfare. Alex shoved the magazine and report card under her shirt. "Alex Russo, your exam results plus the homework—" the card said in a muffled voice.

"What did you say, Alex?" her father asked, looking at her curiously.

Alex couldn't see any easy way out. She had no choice. She'd have to eat the evidence.

She ripped off a piece of the report card, shoved it in her mouth, and began to chew. "Nothing," she answered her father.

"Alex, it's not very ladylike to talk with your mouth full," her mother reminded her.

Alex chewed faster. The paper certainly tasted different than her dad's famous hoagies. But when she opened her mouth again, out flew the report card, completely whole.

"What's that?" her father asked, pointing to the card hovering in the air.

Alex's eyes widened. She was *so* busted. Unless . . . She whipped a magic wand out of her sleeve and pointed it toward her parents. *"These parents are now not—"* she began to chant.

"What are you doing?" her father asked, trying to interrupt her spell.

"*Two guinea pigs should fill their slot!*" Alex finished.

Lights suddenly began to flash. Alex closed her eyes. When she opened them again, she couldn't believe what she was seeing. She had just turned her mother and father into guinea pigs! Her now small furry parents twitched their noses at her.

Well, at least I got the spell right this time, Alex thought. But now what?

Chapter Three

A little while later, Alex's brothers returned home. Justin held the apartment door open with his shoulder as he tried to balance a big, brown grocery bag filled with chips, dips, and soda. Max teetered in behind him. He was carrying an enormous box that was basically the same size as he was.

"I still don't know why you'd spend your entire savings on a giant exercise ball," Justin said to Max, who was hidden behind the box.

Max dropped the box onto the floor and peered closer at the photo on the front of it. "It's for exercise? I was going to blow this up and walk across the ocean in it," he said, disappointed.

"That *is* exercise, Max." Justin walked to the kitchen and began unpacking his groceries.

"Aw, man," Max groaned. He had thought the clear plastic ball sounded like fun. Exercise sounded like work.

Just then Alex wandered in from the terrace. She held a large wire cage covered by a yellow towel.

Max peeked inside. "Cool, guinea pigs!" he exclaimed. "Can I race them?"

"No." Alex pulled the cage out of Max's reach. "I'm still working on Dad's transfiguration spell, and these guinea pigs have to stay in their cage no matter what."

"Fine. I'll just go ask Mom and Dad." Max smirked and headed toward his parents' bedroom.

Alex gulped. "Mom and Dad aren't here because they went to an emergency sandwich-shop convention," she said, thinking fast.

"Emergency sandwich-shop convention?" Justin asked curiously.

"Yeah." Alex knew that the key to fibbing was believing the story you were telling, no matter how crazy it was. If you sounded confident, people usually went along with you. "You know how you were all tweaked because sandwich wraps are really tortillas, and they don't get enough credit? Well, people are finally getting behind that."

"Yes! My e-mail campaign worked!" Justin cheered. Satisfied, he picked up a bowl of chips and salsa to take into the family room. "Now get out of here, you guys. I'm having my AP biology friends over to watch the new episode of *Volcano Discovery* in high-definition. And I don't want you guys to embarrass me."

"*We* are not the embarrassing part of

what you just said," Alex replied.

Justin glared at her and headed over to the couch.

Alex breathed a sigh of relief. Her brothers didn't suspect a thing. Things were still normal. Well—almost normal. Now she just needed to figure out how to turn these rodents back into her parents!

"That was the best volcano special ever," Justin's friend Zack said about an hour later. Seven kids from their biology class were gathered around the television in the family room. "The high-def made it seem like the volcano was right in your living room."

Justin, sitting next to Zack on the sofa, nodded. "Which, geologically speaking, would be a statistical improbability along the lines of there being a snowstorm in the Saharan desert," he said with a laugh.

Zack started laughing, too. The only bigger

science geek than Justin in their high school was Zack. "You got me! Good nerd burn."

Just then, Alex came down the circular staircase. She was carrying a large shovel and a blue plastic bucket. "Well, I'm off to the park to bury something," she announced. Then she noticed her report card peeking out of the bucket. She pushed it down, out of sight, and headed toward the front door.

Zack perked up. "Oh, a time capsule?"

"Yeah, sure," Alex said, trying to rush out the door. She really needed to get rid of her report card!

"I love doing that!" Justin exclaimed. "You should put a cell phone in it, call it, and leave a voice mail. So that way someone in the future can pick it up."

"Actually, people take my calls *now*," Alex said. Maybe she wasn't the smartest Russo, but she definitely was the most social. She opened the door to find her best friend, Harper, standing posed in the doorway. Harper was pretty dressed up for a visit with Alex. She also looked as if she'd been waiting there for a while.

"Harper, what are you doing here?" Alex asked, surprised.

"I heard about Justin's big party, and I've been working up the nerve to crash it," she replied. It was no secret that she had a huge crush on Alex's older brother.

"Oh. Well, I've been working up the nerve to leave." Alex stepped past Harper. "Oh, look! I did it," she said, and shut the door behind her.

"Hey, everyone," Harper chirped, opening the door and entering the living room. She perched herself on the edge of the sofa. "So, volcanoes, huh? That's a *hot* topic. Am I right?" She giggled at her own joke. The other kids stared silently at her. "Volcanoes, they're *hot*," she repeated and laughed. No one else joined in.

"We're off volcanoes," Zack informed her.

Harper blushed. She had been working on volcano jokes for the last twenty minutes. She didn't have any other material ready.

"Now we're debating who's smarter, a twelve-year-old boy or a common guinea pig," Zack told her.

"Ooh, I'm on Justin's side!" Harper said enthusiastically. Then she paused. "Which side are you on, Justin?"

"As always, I'm on the side of science," Justin said, walking to the kitchen. He lifted up the cage of guinea pigs. "This calls for an experiment."

A little while later, everyone had made their way downstairs to the empty Waverly Sub Station. The boys pushed the tables and chairs out of the way as Justin set up the experiment.

Both guinea pigs scurried about inside a small, plastic running ball, which spun as their little feet pattered on the inside.

At the same time, Max stood inside his own inflated plastic ball. The balls were placed side by side at a starting line that had been marked on the floor with duct tape.

"This was so totally worth my allowance. I'm going to use it forever," Max called from inside his plastic bubble.

"Okay. When Harper says 'go,' you'll both try and make your way to the stack of cheese slices located outside the subway car," Justin instructed. The restaurant was decorated to look like an actual subway, and had a few old subway cars for people to sit in. He pointed to Zack, who stood on the opposite side of the restaurant, holding a plate of cheese slices.

Harper positioned herself in front of the contestants. She raised her pink scarf in the air, as if she were standing on a race track. "Three . . . two . . . one . . . go!" She waved the scarf valiantly.

The guinea pigs pumped their little legs. Their plastic ball spun forward, rolling toward the cheese.

Max tried to sprint, sending his huge plastic ball careening sideways. It ricocheted off the wall. Max tripped, falling down inside the ball. "I hate this thing," he grumbled.

The guinea pigs, in their clear plastic ball, rolled across the floor. The kids cheered as it picked up speed. It spun faster and faster. Suddenly, the ball crashed full-force into the wall next to Zack! The plastic ball split open and the guinea pigs ran out.

"Alex's guinea pigs are getting away! Catch them!" Justin called.

His friends ran in every direction trying to catch them, but the furry creatures were long gone.

"Oh, man. We lost Alex's guinea pigs. I knew if I had a party without parental supervision this would get out of hand," Justin groaned.

"Oh, Alex is going to freak out," Max said from inside his plastic bubble. Then he had an idea. "Unless we buy two more guinea pigs at the pet store."

"Good thinking," Justin said as he held up the empty cage. "Um, let's hide this so Alex doesn't find it."

"And then we'll go to the pet store. They always give me a treat," Max said.

"Those are dog biscuits," Justin said, a look of disgust on his face.

"I know. What do you think keeps my teeth so white and my hair so shiny?" Max remarked.

Justin rolled his eyes and then glanced at the empty cage. He sure hoped their plan would work!

Chapter Four

Meanwhile, Alex sat on the edge of the velvet sofa in the wizard lair. She stared at the report card that just wouldn't go away. Her earlier plan to bury it had backfired, and she was running out of ideas.

"Look, you change into a C now, and I promise I'll get an A next semester. And it'll all even out," she bargained.

"Sorry!" the report card sang out.

Alex groaned. "Then you leave me no

choice." She flipped the switch to the paper shredder she had set up on the floor by the sofa. She pushed the report card in the slot. She hoped that maybe the shredder would work better than the garbage disposal that she had thought would do the trick earlier.

Just then, ribbons of paper slid out. Presto!

Suddenly, a hazy smoke filled the room and the floor-to-ceiling window swung open wide. Professor Crumbs glided in—and he didn't look pleased.

"Alex Russo," he announced, "you haven't returned your wizard report card."

"Wow! Talk about a paper cut," said another voice. Alex whirled around. It was her report card! It was whole again—and sitting on the sofa. Alex gasped.

She flew into action and grabbed the report card before it could speak again. Then she dashed over to a huge leather-bound book of spells that rested on a side table. She opened the cover, slipped the report card inside, and shut the book tightly. She pushed her palm down hard on the book cover. The report card squirmed under the weight of her hand, but she wasn't lifting it. Not for anything. There was no way that card was going to escape!

"I need to speak to your parents straightaway," Professor Crumbs said.

Alex hoped he couldn't see her hand on the book. "Um, could you just give me one minute?" she asked nervously.

She looked around, unsure of what to do, when she noticed the hidden guinea pig cage on the floor. She knelt down, her palm still pressing the book closed, and peeked under the yellow towel. Oh, no! The guinea pigs were missing!

Alex turned toward Professor Crumbs. "Actually, my parents took my report card with them to a sandwich-shop convention. I'm sure you're familiar with the tortilla–versus–

sandwich-wrap controversy."

Professor Crumbs stared blankly at her.

"No? Okay." Now what? she wondered. She pressed her hand down harder on the book, trying to come up with something—anything!

But suddenly, Professor Crumbs spoke. "I agree," he said, stroking his long white beard. "Tortillas were cheated." He seemed deep in thought. "I can see why your parents dove into this most pressing crisis. I'm sorry I questioned you. Will you accept my apology?"

Alex smiled. He had fallen for it—just like Justin had! "Definitely. Thanks for stopping by. Don't be a stranger." She could feel the report card wiggling under the cover of the book, desperately trying to escape. "Say hi to the little warlocks for me." She put all her weight on her hand.

"Let's wizard-handshake on it," Professor Crumbs suggested. He crossed his arms in front of him and held out both hands.

Alex stared in disbelief. "The . . . the two-handed wizard handshake?" she asked uncertainly. There was no way she could do that *and* keep the book cover closed.

"That's the one." He extended his arms toward her.

Maybe if I sit on the book and shake hands really, really fast, she thought. One . . . two . . . three . . . She sat on the book and reached out her hands. Then something bit her!

"Ow!" Alex cried, jumping away.

"The only thing she gets an A in is hiding and lying!" the report card yelled out. It bounced up and down excitedly on the table.

"Be still," Professor Crumbs said to the report card. He grabbed it and pinched it closed, silencing it. Then he turned to Alex. "You lied to me," he said quietly.

"I can explain," Alex offered.

"I'm not interested in what you have to

say anymore. I'm coming back tonight to see your parents, and we'll decide how long to suspend your powers." He slipped the report card into a pocket in his black robe.

"My powers? No! You can't! I'm going to need those." Alex knew her powers were essential if she wanted any shot at getting herself out of this mess and turning her parents back to normal. "I'm also going to need to know a sound that someone could make to attract . . . a guinea pig, for instance," Alex said, trying to stall him.

Professor Crumbs looked intrigued. "Oh, I would try a sort of rabbit-y thing, but with more saliva." He scrunched up his nose and made rodentlike sounds.

Alex mimicked the sounds he made. Then she tried them in a louder voice.

"Desist," Professor Crumbs said, suddenly realizing that Alex had led him offtrack. "You haven't acted with any responsibility. Say good-bye to your magical ability," he said in a serious tone.

He pointed toward Alex. The air crackled with electricity. Energy seemed to flow from Professor Crumbs to Alex and back again. Alex felt as if all the air was being vacuumed from her body. Suddenly, a ball of electricity formed in Professor Crumbs's hands, and Alex realized that the colorful orb of sparkling light contained her magical powers.

"No!" Alex cried. Without her powers, how would she ever be able to fix things?

Chapter Five

Back from the pet store, Max circled the cage of new guinea pigs in the living room. He peered closely at them. Furry. Little, pudgy bodies. Twitchy noses. "Okay, these guinea pigs look just like the ones we lost," he told Justin.

"You think these will trick Alex?" Justin asked. He'd had some trouble in the pet store remembering the exact coloring of the original guinea pigs.

Suddenly, Alex stormed upstairs from the lair and into the family room. She couldn't believe that Professor Crumbs had taken her powers away! She was caught up in her own thoughts, until she saw her brothers staring into the cage with worried looks on their faces. "What are you doing with my guinea pigs?" she demanded.

Alex held the cage and stared into the round, black eyes of the furry creatures. She felt pretty guilty. She knew she had to tell her brothers the truth. "Mom and Dad aren't really away for the weekend," she confessed. "I had to turn them into these guinea pigs to keep them from seeing my grades."

"So, the guinea pigs in the cage . . . were actually *Mom and Dad*," Justin said slowly, the realization of all that had happened sinking in.

"Yeah, these guinea pigs are Mom and Dad," Alex replied.

"No, 'were,'" Justin said, suddenly looking panicked. "Because they scurried off, so we bought these at the pet store!" he exclaimed.

Max sunk down into the sofa. He put his head into his hands.

"Oh, man!" Max cried.

"How could you do something so stupid?" Alex yelled. She couldn't believe her brothers had lost their parents!

"Only a stupid person would think that my stupid thing was stupider than your stupid thing!" Justin countered. "You don't even *deserve* to have wizard powers, Alex," Justin said, clearly not knowing what had just happened with Professor Crumbs.

"Look, this isn't about me right now. This is about finding Mom and Dad," Alex said, trying to remain calm.

"Who you turned into guinea pigs!" Justin reminded her angrily.

"Okay, it's a *little* about me," Alex agreed.

"Here's what we should do. We'll ask these guinea pigs where guinea pigs would run away to."

Justin glared at his sister and pointed toward the cage. "How are we going to ask these guinea pigs *anything*?"

"Well . . . use the transfiguration spell to turn them into people, and then they'll be able to tell us," Alex said. If Justin had been able to turn a guinea pig into a dove, and Alex had been able to turn her parents into guinea pigs, surely they could do *this*.

"*You* use it. It's your problem," Justin said, annoyed.

Alex grimaced. Time for one more confession. "I can't. Professor Crumbs suspended my powers until Mom and Dad sign my report card."

"*What?*" Justin raised his arms in exasperation. "Is there *anything* else you want to tell me?"

"Yeah," Alex admitted. "There's no emergency

sandwich-shop convention. Nobody cares about your tortilla movement."

Justin gasped. Now he was really mad. He started to leave the room.

"No! Justin, look!" Alex cried, reaching for his arm to stop him. "Will you just hurry and say the spell, please?"

Justin sighed. He *did* want his parents back. "Fine," he said as he pulled his wand out of his sleeve. Then he placed the cage on the floor. He pointed his wand at the rodents and chanted, *"These guinea pigs are small, dumb, and hairy. Make them human to find Theresa and Jerry."*

Bright light flashed from his wand and zapped the cage. All of a sudden, a man and a woman appeared where the guinea pigs had once been.

"You've got to be kidding me! We're human!" the woman cried. The once–guinea pig looked like a real human. Well, *almost*. She wore a bright green dress, but she still had pointy rodent ears, buck teeth, and a twitchy nose.

The man checked out his new human form in amazement. A white suit with a black bow tie was stretched over his pudgy body. He stared at his hands. "I'm going to use my opposable thumb to pick stuff up!" he exclaimed, clearly excited.

Then the man grabbed a vase and a statue off a side table and waved the objects in the air. "Check it out! I have things in both hands!"

"Okay, settle down," Alex instructed. "We need your help finding a couple of guinea pigs, guinea people."

The guinea-pig man and woman began sniffing and circling each other in a frenzy.

"Oh! I smell peanut butter and jelly crusts!" the woman cried.

"And dirty socks!" the man exclaimed. He sniffed again. "And orange soda!"

Alex looked at Justin. Justin looked at Alex.

"Under Max's bed!" they said together.

They raced up the spiral staircase and down the hall to Max's bedroom.

"Ew!" Justin exclaimed as they entered the room. To call Max's bedroom a mess would have be too kind. Garbage dumps looked—and smelled—much better.

Alex searched for empty spots of floor under the piles of unidentifiable junk. Justin started across the room, when he felt something attach itself to his pants leg. He glanced down and almost gagged. He pulled off a paper plate piled high with a sticky green and gray glob. "Is this marshmallows smeared on asparagus?" he asked, completely disgusted.

"Yes. Yes, it is, Justin." Max grabbed the plate from his brother and held it delicately. "That experiment is almost complete."

"Max, what are you doing with Mom's black dress?" Alex asked, holding up a long dress that had been crumpled on the floor.

Max snatched the dress from her hands. "It's a Darth Vader cape," he said defensively. "You people have no imagination."

Alex and Justin tiptoed over the piles of junk to the bed and knelt down to peer underneath the bed.

"*This* is where my lucky mug went!" Justin shouted. He reached past the giant balls of dust and half-eaten sandwiches to retrieve it.

"There they are!" Alex announced. She pointed farther under the bed. Two guinea pigs sat side by side, staring straight out at Alex and her brother.

"Hi, Mom. Hi, Dad," Alex said to the guinea pigs. Then she looked closer. Was it possible? Did the animals have expressions of *anger* on their faces? She turned to Justin. "Oh, they look mad. Maybe changing them back is a bad idea."

"Yeah, it's a bad idea," Justin said sarcastically. "Let's just be raised by two guinea pigs!"

"Oh," Alex said, seeing his point. Suddenly, the guinea pigs tried to make a run for it. Alex jumped up and chased them across the room. They darted into the closet, and Alex slammed the door shut.

"Okay." Justin stood and pulled out his wand. He pointed it toward the closet. *"These guinea pigs are now not. Mom and Dad should fill their slot!"* he chanted.

Just then, the closet door burst open. Back in human form, Mr. Russo barreled out. Mrs. Russo was right behind him. Neither of them looked amused.

"Alex Russo, you are in *so* much trouble!" her dad bellowed.

"Look, I can explain. But first you guys need to know that Professor Crumbs is coming to discuss my horrible report card with you," Alex said quickly.

And just like that, Professor Crumbs magically appeared in Max's room.

"Mr. and Mrs. Russo," Professor Crumbs began to say, "I am here—" A loud squishing noise interrupted his speech. He gazed down at his shoe, disgusted. "What am I standing on?"

Max stepped forward and pulled a gooey substance off the bottom of the headmaster's shoe. "Um, it's marshmallow surprise. The surprise is the asparagus," he explained.

"Alex, do you want to tell Professor Crumbs where we were?" her father asked.

Alex turned to the headmaster. "I turned them into guinea pigs to keep them from seeing my report card," she admitted.

"Hmm." The headmaster seemed to be thinking about her deception. "And how did that work out for you?" he asked.

"Not well." She stared at the floor. I've really done it this time, she thought.

"Oh, I see you have Alex's powers," Mr. Russo said, pointing to the electric orb the headmaster was holding. "Don't let them fall into the wrong hands. Oh, wait, they *were* in the wrong hands," he joked.

"Yes, they were," Professor Crumbs said. But he wasn't laughing. "I am taking away her powers forever. I have never seen such a blatant disregard for the student-wizard code of conduct," he said sternly.

"No! No! No! Please don't do this. I've come this far. It's not fair!" Alex protested.

"I'm afraid it is," the headmaster said. "I shall take your powers and be on my way." He went to tuck the orb inside his robe when a flash of orange light suddenly zapped him.

Alex gasped. The headmaster was now a furry guinea pig!

"Professor Crumbs turned into a guinea pig! Sweet!" Max cried.

Alex noticed her parents glaring at her. "Don't look at *me*," she said. "I don't have my powers."

Then everyone noticed Justin standing in the corner—with his magic wand raised.

"*Justin?*" Mr. Russo said in disbelief.

Justin shrugged. "I panicked," he explained.

Alex couldn't believe her goody-two-shoes brother had turned the headmaster of Wiz Tech into a guinea pig just for her! She was seriously impressed . . . until she started to feel guilty. "This is my problem, not yours," she told her brother. "Don't let me drag you down."

"But you don't drag me down," Justin said. "I don't want you to lose your powers. Every time you mess up, I have to think of a way to fix it. You make me a better wizard," he explained.

Mr. Russo shook his head. "Look, I don't know. Professor Crumbs as a guinea pig?" This was *bad*. "Somebody's going to lose their powers. Justin, you have to change him back," he said.

Justin gulped. His father was right. He pointed his wand at the guinea pig, cleared his throat, and said the reversal spell. *"This guinea pig is a bad dresser. Turn him now into my professor."*

Blue and green light flashed from Justin's wand, and Professor Crumbs reappeared. He seemed fine, although still a bit twitchy.

"Justin Russo! How dare you! You are supposed to be a model student. I'm appalled!" the headmaster scolded.

"I know. I deserve whatever punishment you're about to give me," Justin said.

Alex stepped forward. "Professor, this is all my fault," she confessed. She couldn't let Justin take the fall for her mess.

"Justin, I heard what you said about your sister through my guinea-pig ears," Professor Crumbs said.

Alex locked eyes with Justin. Oh, no!

"And if you could do something like that, I

can't ignore it," he continued. "You two bring out the best in each other. Alex, I know I'm going to regret this, but I am returning your powers so you can train alongside your brothers."

With that, Professor Crumbs pulled out the electric orb and magically transported it back into Alex. Alex smiled. Her powers were back! She was a wizard again.

"I'll see you in my office Monday morning at eight o'clock," the headmaster said to her, and with that, he magically vanished.

"Alex, is there something you want to say to your brother?" Mr. Russo hinted.

"Yeah." Alex moved closer to Justin. "Thanks for sticking up for me," she said sincerely.

"Yeah." Justin blushed. He and Alex were rarely nice to each other in front of other people. "Professor Crumbs really bought that story I laid onto him about you making me a better wizard."

"Yeah. I really hate you." Alex smiled.

Justin grinned. "Yeah. I hate you, too."

"And I guess if it means so much to you, I'll sign your tortilla petition," Alex offered.

"Thank you," Justin replied happily.

"Well, I really hate *both* of you," Max piped up. "Now we don't have *any* guinea pigs!"

Alex was sure there was a spell to fix that. Now that she had her powers back, she might as well put them to good use. How much more trouble could she possibly get into, anyway?

She reached for her wand. I guess we'll find out! she thought.

Something magical is on the way!
Look for the next book in Disney's
Wizards of Waverly Place series.

Rev It Up!

Adapted by N. B. Grace

Based on the series created by Todd J. Greenwald

Part One is based on the episode "Racing," Written by Justine Bateman

Part Two is based on the episode "Taxi Dance," Written by Peter Murrieta

The halls of Tribeca Prep were filled with students rushing to their next class or grabbing books from their lockers. Everyone seemed to have a purpose—something to do or somewhere to go.

Everyone, that is, except Alex Russo. She wandered aimlessly through the hall, her dark brown eyes fixed on a small group of boys who were standing in a circle and talking.

Unfortunately, she was so focused on watching the group that she wasn't paying attention to where she was going—something she realized when she accidentally slammed into two other students, knocking their books right out of their hands.

Alex shrugged a quick apology and scurried over to her best friend, Harper Evans, who was standing by a row of lockers. As usual, Harper, who prided herself on her fashion flair, was dressed in one of her outlandish outfits. Today, she was wearing a light pink ruffled shirt, a flowered skirt, a striped scarf, and a bright pink hair bow.

But Alex didn't have time right then to comment on Harper's creative outfit. "Is he looking at me?" Alex asked her friend urgently. "Is he looking at me?"

Harper narrowed her eyes as she gazed at the group of boys Alex had been staring at, which included Dean Moriarti, Alex's latest crush. "No," Harper reported. "Walk by again."

Alex rolled her eyes. "I can't. That will be my fifth time. He'll think I'm lost." She sighed. "How am I going to figure out if he likes me?"

Harper shook her head in disbelief. "Why is this so hard for you?"

"Because he knows I like him, and I don't know how he feels about me!" Alex explained impatiently. "I've never been in this position before."

"That's why I always play it cool around Justin," Harper said confidently. She had a major crush on Alex's older brother. "I don't want him to know I like him."

Suddenly, Harper's eyes widened as she saw Justin Russo standing at his locker. "Oh, there he is!" she squealed. She lunged toward him in excitement. "Hi, Justin!" she said brightly. "I was wondering if you wanted to come over today, because I rented three DVDs, and they're not due back until Monday, and I think two of them are really good," she said, talking a mile a minute. So much for playing it cool!

Justin was very aware that Harper had a massive crush on him, so he knew how to handle this. He grabbed his sunglasses out of his locker, put them on, and then strode past her as quickly as possible.

Harper was undaunted. "All right, I'll talk to you later about it! Bye!" she called out to Justin's back as he walked away.

Flushed and smiling, she turned her attention back to Alex, who was looking at her with raised eyebrows.

"Yeah, I can't play it cool like *you*, Harper," Alex said sarcastically.

Then she returned to thinking about her own dilemma. After a few moments, Alex came to a decision. "Look, I'm just going to go up to him, talk to him, and see if he likes me."

Before she could lose her courage, she strode over to where Dean and his friends were standing. "Hey, Dean," Alex said, trying to sound casual.

Dean smiled at her. "What's up, Russo?"

Before she could answer, Dean's friend Joey interrupted. "Hey, Dean!" he said excitedly. "We got the full story on that sweet ride. The one for the race at Paramus."

Alex didn't know what they were talking about—except that Paramus was a city in New Jersey—but she poked her head in between two of the boys and tried to join in the conversation.

"Uh, sounds great!" she said enthusiastically.

"Joey's getting the story on this car we might run," Dean explained. "Hey, tell it, Joey."

Alex poked her head over someone's shoulder. "Yeah, tell it, Joey," she encouraged him.

She turned back to grin at Harper. Her friend frowned and pointed at the group of boys to signal to Alex that she needed to be paying attention to *them*.

Alex nodded and rushed around the circle to see if she could find another opening.

"So, they had to rebuild," Joey was saying. "It was completely greasy and . . . and . . ."

Dean didn't need to hear the rest of that sentence—he knew what it meant. "The car's not going to be ready in time, boys," he said, shaking his head.

His friends groaned. Alex wasn't sure exactly what the problem was, but she could tell that the news was grim.

She pushed her way into the center of the circle. "Oh, bummer; that stinks," she said . . . a little too late.

The boys all stared at her. She gulped and slipped back outside the circle, embarrassed. Harper gave her a sympathetic look.

"And I'll bet they attached the Edelbrock heads and then ordered a new Milodon pan and timing cover," Dean continued.

Confused and discouraged, Alex ran back over to Harper, ready to give up. But Harper shook her head and pointed back at Dean, then shooed Alex away.

Alex rolled her eyes, but she knew Harper was right. After all, a football player didn't quit the field after getting tackled one time, a basketball player didn't stop playing after one missed shot! She was determined to figure out if Dean liked her—and the only way to do that was to get back in the game!